This Walker book belongs to:

. . . .

. . . .

. . . .

To my wife

First published in Great Britain 2011 by Walker Books Ltd
87 Vauxhall Walk, London SE11 5HJ

10 9 8 7 6 5 4 3 2 1

Copyright © 2010 Mo Willems

First published in the United States 2010 by Balzer + Bray,
an imprint of HarperCollins Children's Books.
British publication rights arranged with
Sheldon Fogelman Agency, Inc.

This book has been typeset in Typography of Coop

Printed in China

British Library Cataloguing in Publication Data:
a catalogue record for this book is available
from the British Library.

ISBN 978-1-4063-3649-8

www.walker.co.uk

Knuffle Bunny Free

AN UNEXPECTED DIVERSION BY **Mo Willems**

WALKER BOOKS
AND SUBSIDIARIES
LONDON · BOSTON · SYDNEY · AUCKLAND

One day, not so long ago,
Trixie took a big trip with her family.

They were on their way to visit Trixie's "Oma" and "Opa" in Holland.

Holland is far away.

So that meant taking
a taxi to the airport,

watching Knuffle Bunny
go through the big machine,

queuing up.

waiting some more,

and (finally) getting on to a real aeroplane!

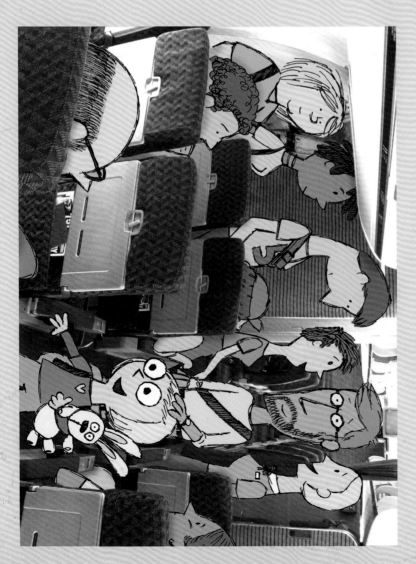

On the plane,
Trixie played

and read

and slept.

Before she knew it, the plane had landed.

Trixie and her family left the airport and got on a train to go to …

Oma and Opa's house!

Oma and Opa were so happy to see Trixie!

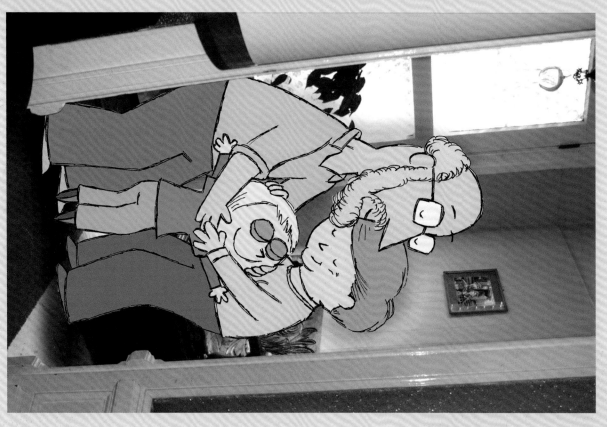

Soon Oma and Trixie were drinking cold glasses of chocolate milk in the garden.

Suddenly Trixie realized something!

Trixie didn't tell her daddy that Knuffle Bunny was gone.

She didn't have to.

Trixie's daddy called the airline and asked them to look for Knuffle Bunny on the plane.

But the plane had left for

China.

China is very far away...

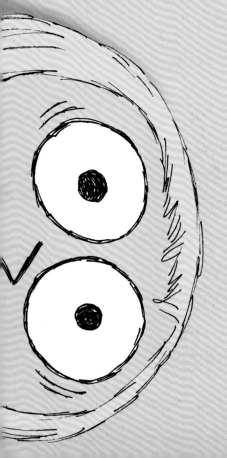

Trixie's daddy told the story of when he was a little boy and said goodbye to his "Special Lamby".

Trixie's mummy hugged her and asked her to be brave.

Oma gave Trixie another glass of chocolate milk and remarked on how big she was getting.

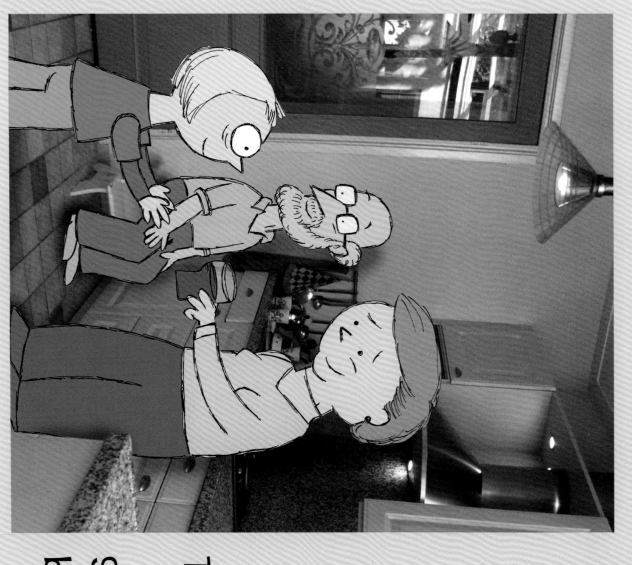

Trixie understood.

She was getting bigger.

The next morning, Trixie tried to enjoy going to the café

and the
swings in the
playground

and the carnival
that was in town.

And while the whole week was filled with fun things, like eating chips on the street,

visiting real windmills and feeding the ducks,

Trixie was still sad.

She missed her Knuffle Bunny.

(Oma and Opa understood.)

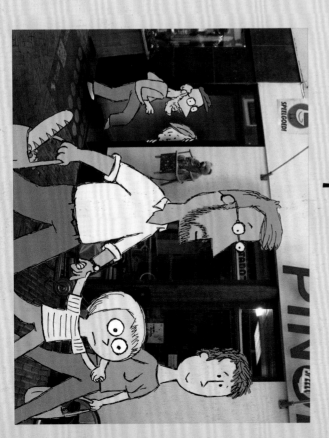

(Oma and Opa had a plan.)

That night, they had a surprise for Trixie: a brand-new top-of-the-range

FUNNY-BUNNY-WUNNY-DOLL WUNNY-BUNNY-DOLL™ EXTREME!

She played with Oma on the playground swings.

Trixie had a big breakfast.

The next morning,
Trixie felt better.

She dreamed of how Knuffle Bunny would make them feel better.

She even tried a sip of Opa's coffee at the café!

It was a great day.

Before she knew it, the trip was over and it was time to go home.
Trixie hugged Oma and Opa as hard as she could.

and back on to the plane,

Then Trixie and her family
got back on to the train,

and listened to the crying baby as the plane lifted off.

But can you believe it?
Right there, on that very plane,

Trixie noticed something...

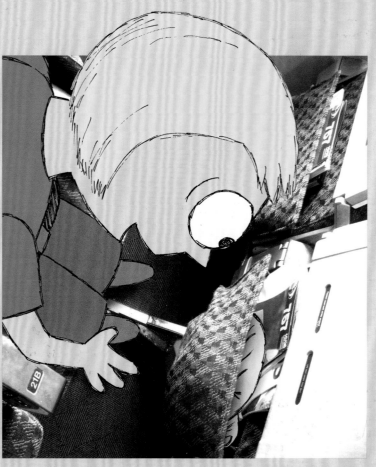

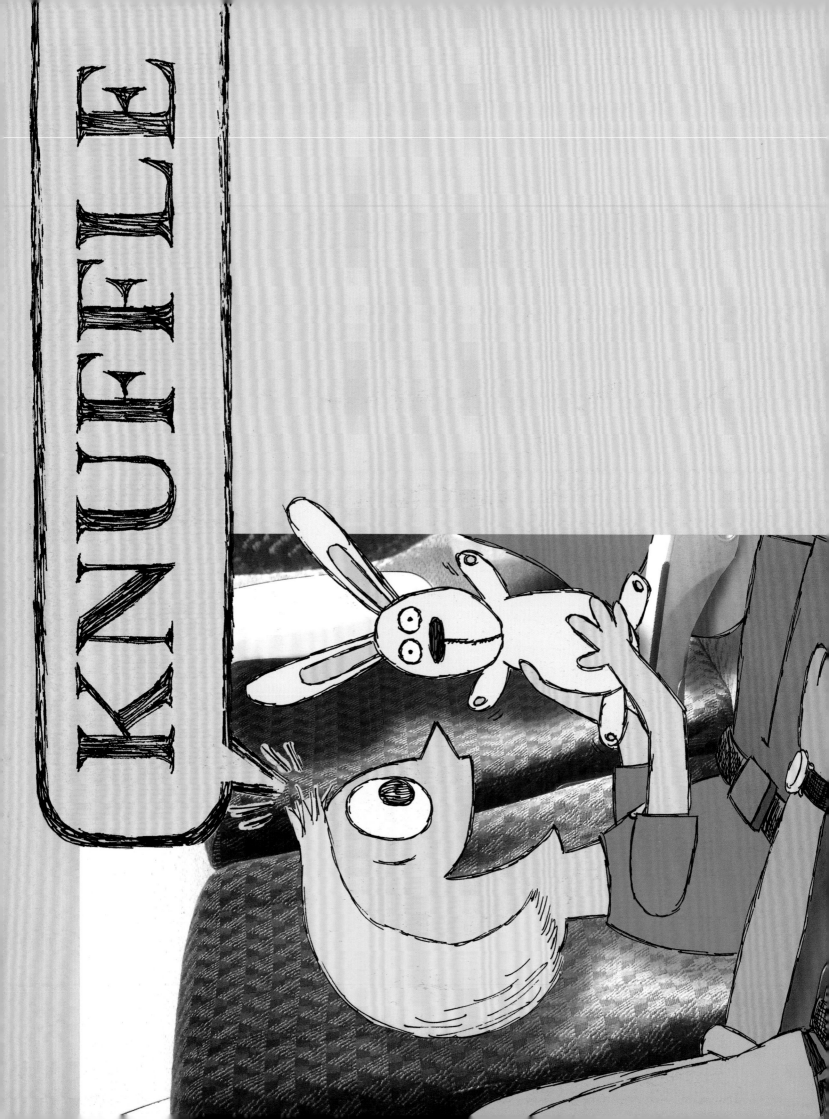

KNUFFLE

BUNNY!!!

Trixie was so happy to have Knuffle Bunny back in her arms.

Trixie turned round and said:

Would your baby like my Knuffle Bunny?

WAAA!

Happy enough to make a decision...

said Trixie. She was big enough.

The baby was happy.
The baby's mother was thankful.
Trixie's parents were proud.

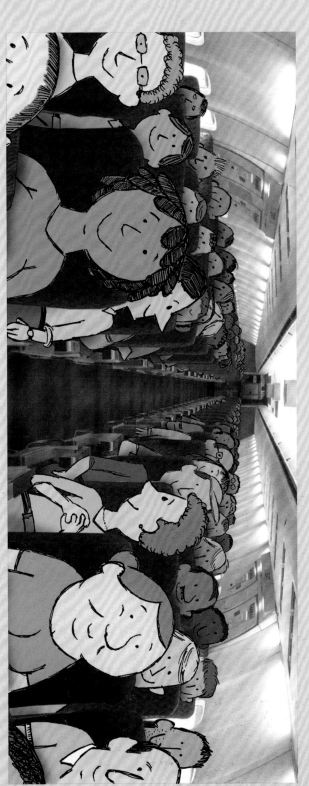

And the other passengers
were very relieved.

a few weeks later,

And that is how,

The end.

A NOTE TO TRIXIE:

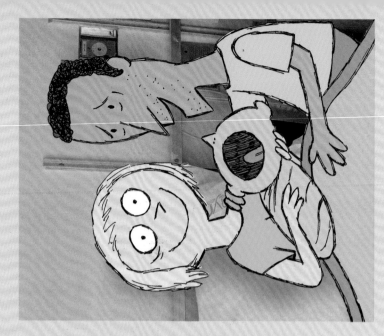

START A FAMILY
AND BE HAPPY.

FALL IN LOVE,

TRIXIE, I HOPE TO WATCH
YOU GROW UP,

AND I HOPE THAT ONE DAY, MANY YEARS FROM NOW,

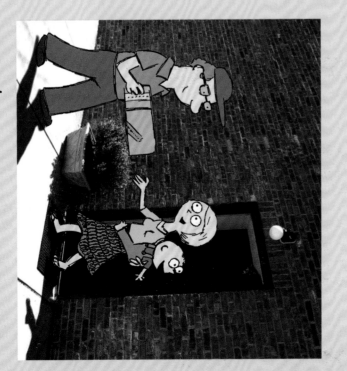

YOU WILL RECEIVE A PACKAGE

. . . FROM AN OLD PEN PAL.

LOVE,
DADDY

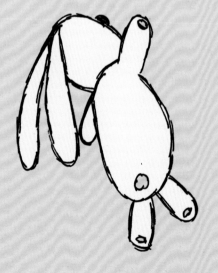

Special thanks to:

Rob Gussenhoven, American Airlines, the Port Authority of

NY & NJ, the TSA, Ambassador Scieszka, the Lewine family,

Giorgio Balzer, the real Oma, Opa, Mummy and especially Trixie.

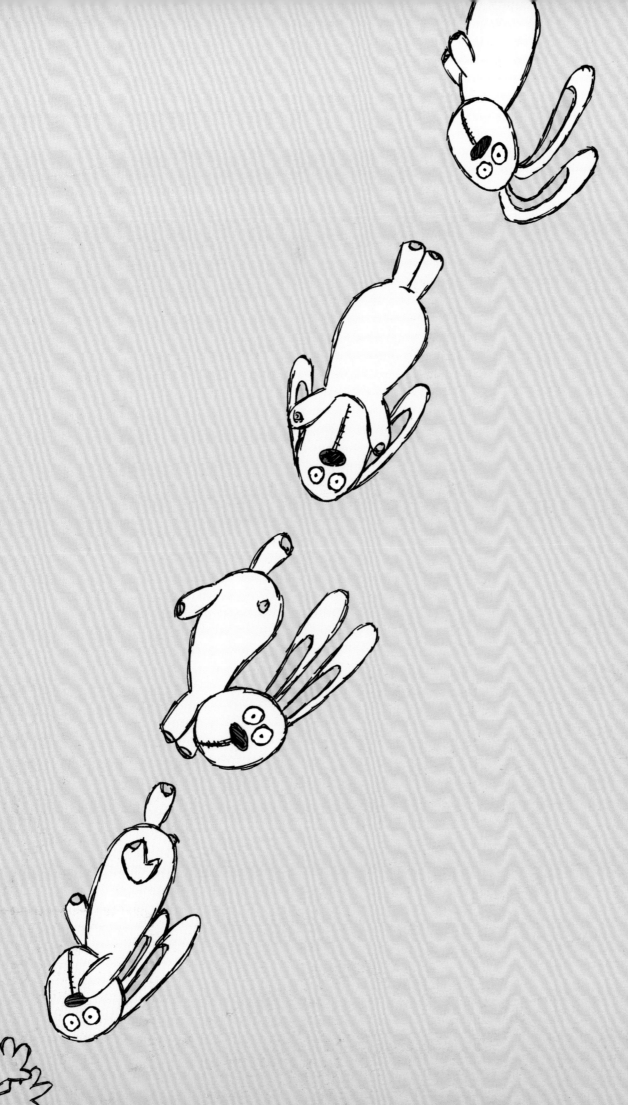

Mo Willems is the renowned author of many award-winning picture books, including the Caldecott Honor winners *Don't Let the Pigeon Drive the Bus!*, *Knuffle Bunny* and *Knuffle Bunny Too*. About *Knuffle Bunny Free* Mo says,

"In the previous books, the parents made the decisions for Trixie, they made things happen ... but in this book, Trixie makes the decision on her own. And it's really beautiful to see." Before making picture books, Mo was a writer and animator on *Sesame Street*, where he won six Emmys. Mo lives with his family in Massachusetts, USA.

Visit him online at www.mowillems.com and www.GoMo.net

Previous Knuffle Bunny books:

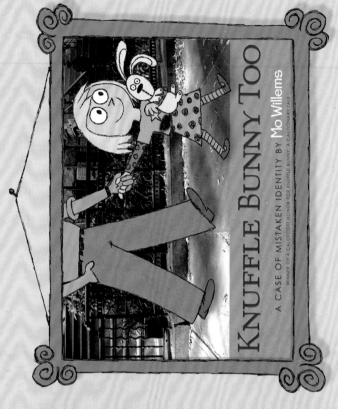

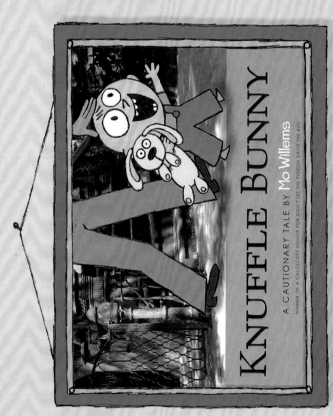

Available from all good bookshops